Norman Gale

Songs for Little People

Norman Gale

Songs for Little People

ISBN/EAN: 9783744768146

Printed in Europe, USA, Canada, Australia, Japan

Cover: Foto ©Andreas Hilbeck / pixelio.de

More available books at **www.hansebooks.com**

SONGS FOR LITTLE PEOPLE

REMEMBERING HER UNCEASING INTEREST

AND ENCOURAGEMENT

I GRATEFULLY DEDICATE THIS BOOK TO

MRS. DENTON, OF RUGBY

NOTE

THIS book is designed for a position between such extremes as the frankly babyish song-books and Stevenson's exquisite and ever-lasting memorials of a child by no means typical. Considering the audience approached, it must be admitted that a few rather difficult words have been allowed entry into the verses; but these have not come by chance, for the author has endeavoured to attract children up to the ages of fourteen and fifteen, as well as those requiring, because of their tenderer years, poems of the simplest sort. Mothers and grown-up sisters or aunts will, it is hoped, translate and explain whenever a young reader appears to be perplexed.

CONTENTS

CONTENTS

viii CONTENTS

THE FAIRY BOOK

IN summer, when the grass is thick, if mother has the
  time,
She shows me with her pencil how a poet makes a
  rhyme,
And often she is sweet enough to choose a leafy nook,
Where I cuddle up so closely when she reads the Fairy-
  book.

In winter, when the corn's asleep, and birds are not in
  song,
And crocuses and violets have been away too long,
Dear mother puts her thimble by in answer to my look,
And I cuddle up so closely when she reads the Fairy-
  book.

A

And mother tells the servants that of course they must
    contrive
To manage all the household things from four till half-
    past five,
For we really cannot suffer interruption from the cook,
When we cuddle close together with the happy Fairy-
    book.

ANGELA'S BIRTH

ANGELA came to us out of the flowers,
God's little blossom that changed into ours.

Cloves for her fingers, and cloves for her toes,
Eyes from the succory, mouth from the rose.

ANGELA'S BIRTH

Loveliness sprang from the sisterly stocks,
Daffodils gave her those yellowy locks.

Fairies that visit her constantly meet
Lilies and lavender making her sweet.

Cherry-pie, pansy, forget-me-not, musk,
Wake in her dawning and sleep in her dusk.

Angela came to us out of the flowers,
God's little blossom that changed into ours.

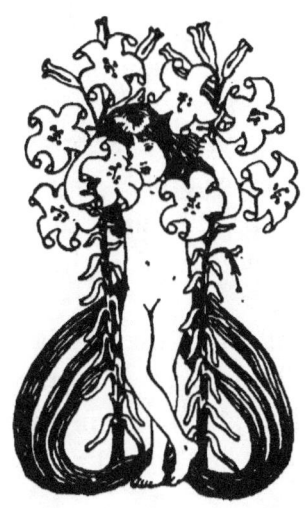

A MIDNIGHT DANCE

THIS boy will tell you, I am sure,
How moon and mouse played on the floor
But he can tell a stranger thing
Of fairy fiddle and magic string.

Nurse says his eyes are far away,
He cannot play as others play ;
And so, perhaps, the fairies came
To cheer him with a midnight game.

His room was full of friendly beams,
Ladders of fancy, light of dreams ;
The moon had placed a shiny hand
On carpet, bed, and washing-stand.

The mouse within the silver lake
Was nibbling crumbs of currant cake,
When thirty fairies bright to see
Appeared in gauzy company.

The girls in sheeny petticoats,
Singing delicious treble notes,
With moving mazes charmed the eye,
Adepts in dance and minstrelsy.

And then came marching from the door,
With steady steps across the floor,
Fairies, made servants for their sins,
With tiny golden violins.

These formed a group beside the bed ;
Each bent his small obedient head,
And then was scraped a dance so sweet
It captured all the hearers' feet.

Oh, how they flitted ! how they leapt !
In magic undulations swept !

And how the fiddlers' fiery bows
Cried FASTER to the tripping toes!

Most rare and lovely was the view—
The twist of red, the flash of blue!
The mouse unfrightened, stared to see
The skipping hues of revelry.

Suddenly stopped the dancing din,
The fiddlers fled, the moon went in:
'Twas thus the kindly fairies came
To show this boy a midnight game.

BARTHOLOMEW

BARTHOLOMEW
Is very sweet,
From sandy hair
To rosy feet.

Bartholomew
Is six months old,
And dearer far
Than pearls or gold.

BARTHOLOMEW

Bartholomew
  Has deep blue eyes,
Round pieces dropped
  From out the skies.

Bartholomew
  Is hugged and kissed!
He loves a flower
  In either fist.

Bartholomew's
  My saucy son:
No mother has
  A sweeter one!

A CHANGE WANTED

It 's very common to be white.
I 'm only just the usual sight.
I 'd like some fairy to employ
To change me into a little black
    boy.

I 'd have my bow and arrows then,
And shoot at stags like grown-up
    men ;
I 'd see the tall giraffe. What joy
To suddenly change to a little
    black boy !

I'd make a football from a gourd,
And get strange birds' eggs for my hoard;
Oh, marvellous must be the toys
That the negroes bring for their little
    black boys!

But I am just the usual sight.
It's very common to be white.
I'd like some fairy to employ
To change me into a little black boy.

THE BUSY FATHER

MOTHER is dead,
   Father is busy ;
He never has time
   For a frolic with Lizzie.

Often he comes,
   Smiling and stilly,
To where she's asleep
   Like the bud of a lily.

Working so hard,
   Worried and busy,
He never has time
   For a frolic with Lizzie.

TUBBING

UNCLE Harry, hear the glee
Coming from the nursery!
Shall we just pop in to see
    Thomas in his tub?

In a soapy pond of joy,
Water as his only toy,
Sits my golden sailor-boy
    Thomas in his tub.

There he is, the little sweet,
Clutching at his rosy feet!
Make your toes and kisses meet
    Thomas in the tub!

Partly come of fairy line,
Partly human, part divine,
How I love this rogue of mine
    Thomas in the tub!

Alf. 15.

THE WINDOW-BOX

O TIMOTHY TROT in the roses and cloves,
So cross if your peas are removed by my doves,
Remember the gift that your favourite loves—
    A window-box full of geraniums.

I 've just had a visit from Doctor Bellairs,
And he says I must lie half a year *for repairs;*
So help me by bringing me quickly upstairs
    A window-box full of geraniums.

I give you, because you are ever so nice,
The cage with the dozen of little white mice,
And all I shall charge is a blossomy price—
    A window-box full of geraniums.

Please tidy my garden for sweet Cousin Bess,
And search in the lupins for snails, and suppress
The weeds for a boy who can only possess
     A window-box full of geraniums.

How often you'll look from the apple-shaped plot
We dug at together, and wish you had got
Your little assistant to carry a pot
     Of musk or sweet-scented geranium!

Perhaps you will cry in the roses and cloves,
Perhaps you will pardon the beaks of my doves;
I know you will bring what your favourite loves—
     A window-box full of geraniums.

THE SPIDER

Boy

SPIDER, spider, come to my call,
Spider, spider, come to my call,
Spider, spider, come to my call
When I bid you, you lazy old spider!

How many flies did you catch yesterday
With your delicate web and its silky display?
Come, tell me the state of your larder, I pray,
You shockingly gluttonous spider.

B

Spider

My web was in luck, for I caught twenty flies
Too near to the earth, but too far from the skies ;
And I bundled them in with the other supplies,
    Like a thrifty and long-headed spider.

Now some were fond lovers, who, buzzing of love,
Looked never around them, below or above,
But popped in my web as a hand to a glove,
    In a manner approved by a spider.

And one is a maiden most lovely to see,
Whose colours betoken a splendid degree ;
She will make a *bonne bouche* for the kind of High
    Tea
    That appeals to the taste of a spider.

But each of the other ones followed a trade,
One served with a needle, one dug with a spade ;
And they're all of them greatly abased, and afraid
    Of their keeper, and eater, the spider.

When feeding-time comes in the cool of the dew,
I shall sup on a plump but a truculent Jew,
Who, because he is caught, makes a pretty to-do
    That provokes all the gorge of a spider.

When Morning arrives with his forehead of gold,
I may breakfast on hot or may breakfast on cold,
On a lad of last night, on a virgin too bold
   Who has tattered the web of the spider.

Boy

   Spider, spider, get you away,
   Spider, spider, get you away,
   Spider, spider, get you away
   When I bid you, you nasty old spider!

HIS FIRST PRAYER

GOD bess Favver,

God bess Muvver,

God bess Sisser,

God bess Bruvver,

God bess Uncoo

Out at sea,

God bess all,

An' God bess me!

MUSTARD AND CRESS

ELIZABETH, my cousin, is the sweetest little girl,
From her eyes like dark blue pansies, to her tiniest
    golden curl ;
I do not use her great long name, but simply call her
    Bess,
And yesterday I planted her in mustard and in cress.

My garden is so narrow that there's very little room,
But I'd rather have her name than get a hollyhock to
    bloom ;
And before she comes to visit us with Charley and with
    Jess,
She'll pop up green and bonny out of mustard and of
    cress.

OUT EARLY

I 'M up in the morning, and over the hill,
Searching the hedges that lead to the mill,
With cook's wicker basket (the small one) to fill,
    Gathering roses for Auntie.

She 's dressing just now, but, of course, little knows
That Tommy, her nephew, is up with the crows,
And, wetting his stockings with dewy drops, goes
    Gathering roses for Auntie.

She 's sweeter than honey ; I love her to come ;
She sings in the passages, brightens the home !
It 's jolly to jump out of bed and to roam
    Gathering roses for Auntie.

As soon as I'm back at the cottage, I mean
To sweeten her plate with these buds cool and clean,
For then she will guess that her nephew has been
    Gathering roses for Auntie.

· BESSIE ·

I 'VE a dove for my cote,
You can hear her soft note;
She sits on the slate
And considers her fate.

And I think she agrees
That a life in the trees
With a spouse rather cross
Is no very great loss.

With corn and with bread
She is tenderly fed;
And only her crop
Need compel her to stop.

I know she is wise,
And there's love in her eyes
When I fill up her pan
Or replenish her can.

She's softer than silk,
With a breast white as milk;
And mother declares
She would like to go shares.

So next Christmas Day
I shall kiss her, and say
That Bessie (the dove)
Is for her, with my love.

TIM'S FOXGLOVE

THERE'S a foxglove, foxglove, foxglove in my garden-
    plot,
Home of yellow-belted bees humming round the spot,
Honey-merchants flying fast from out their dumpy
    cottages
Crowded in companionship by six elm-trees.

There's a foxglove, foxglove, foxglove in my pansy-
    patch,
Decked so brightly by the rain, there never was its
    match ;
Made of petals velvety and russet blots and lovely
    smells,
Shaking dewy clappers in its peal of bells.

There's a foxglove, foxglove, foxglove in my garden-
    ground,
Never mortal listener shall hear its tinkling sound ;
When the stars are tired of dancing, when the elves to
    dreamland creep,
Why, ev'ry bell's a bedroom where the fairies sleep.

THE 'LOGICAL GARDENS

Oh, look from the window, watch the door;
If he comes round the corner, scream and roar!
For Daddy's going to take us four
    On a 'bus to the 'Logical Gardens.

And there the chimpanzee will scratch,
The lions grumble in their patch;
And only fancy! vultures hatch
    Their young in the 'Logical Gardens!

We all shall hear the leopards swear
When keepers feed them in their lair—
Let's buy a bun for the frosty bear
    On his pole in the 'Logical Gardens.

Won't baby have to look up high
When elephants go pounding by
With backs right up against the sky
    In the beautiful 'Logical Gardens?

And there we're all to have our tea,
Not fifty yards from the chimpanzee,
And boa constrictors close will be
    To our cups in the 'Logical Gardens!

And Daddy's promised me and Jake
To stop a keeper and to make
Him show the snake that ate the snake
    For his lunch in the 'Logical Gardens.

Apes captured on the Guinea Coast,
And crested parrots in a host—
There's Daddy by the pillar-post!
    Hurrah for the 'Logical Gardens!

THE HAPPY THRUSH

WHEN Spring, with its sunshine and beauty of bud,
Woke a love in his heart and desire in his voice,
  A comrade he found,
  Of a velvety round,
Whom he courted and won as the bird of his choice.

There's joy and there's pride in the house in the hedge,
For the eggs of last night are a golden-throat clan;
  Five children are born
  In the thick of the thorn,
And the voluble thrush is a Family Man!

THE LOST FRIEND

ALL underneath the restless sea
Grief ran along a wire to me:
Children, your tender friend is gone—
Dear Robert Louis Stevenson.

With radiant smiles he reached his hands
To stroke the young of many lands;
Himself a man and boy in one—
Dear Robert Louis Stevenson.

Since he shall live on children's lips
In tales of treasure and of ships,
What need to raise a tower of stone
For Robert Louis Stevenson?

Samoa nurses him in flowers,
For ever hers, for ever ours ;
Incarnate tune, undying tone,
Dear Robert Louis Stevenson.

THE MAKESHIFT

TIRED, darling?
  Come and rest
That tangled mop
On Auntie's breast!

She does not know
  I have, at best,
A make-believe
  For mother's breast.

Oh, never was
  So sweet a guest
To touch the heart
  In Auntie's breast!

My precious bird,
  Be this thy nest ;
And fall asleep
  On Auntie's breast.

C

CARRYING ANGELA

LEAVING our lodging, I have for a task
    The prettiest, surely, an idler could ask—
Carrying Angela down to the beach,
    A bundle of prattle, and soft as a peach.

Lazily watching the children, I find
    Content for my heart and refreshment of mind,
Making a door in a sandy abode,   .
    Or draining a ditch, or devising a road.

Home then to dinner all laden with shells,
    With curious pebbles and flowering bells ;
Angela rides me, a mistress most fair,
    Her heels at my chest and her fist in my hair.

The · Bad · Boy ·

ONCE a little round-eyed lad
Determined to be very bad.

He called his porridge nasty pap,
And threw it all in nurse's lap.

His gentle sister's cheek he hurt,
He smudged his pinny in the dirt.

He found the bellows, and he blew
The pet canary right in two!

And when he went to bed at night
He would not say his prayers aright.

This pained a lovely twinkling star
That watched the trouble from afar.

She told her bright-faced friends, and soon
The dreadful rumour reached the moon.

The moon, a gossiping old dame,
Told Father Sun the bad boy's shame.

And then the giant sun began
A very satisfactory plan.

Upon the naughty rebel's face
He would not pour his beamy grace.

He would not stroke the dark-brown strands
With entertaining shiny hands.

The little garden of the boy
Seemed desert, missing heaven's joy.

But all his sister's tulips grew
Magnificent with shine and dew.

Where'er he went he found a shade,
But light was poured upon the maid.

He also lost, by his disgrace,
That indoors sun, his mother's face.

His father sent him up to bed
With neither kiss nor pat for head.

And in his sleep he had such foes,
Bad fairies pinched his curling toes—

They bit his ears, they pulled his hairs,
They threw him three times down the stairs.

O little boys who would not miss
A father's and a mother's kiss,

Who would not cause a sister pain,
Who want the sun to shine again,

Who want sweet beams to tend the plot
Where grows the pet forget-me-not,

Who hate a life of streaming eyes,
Be good, be merry, and be wise.

CRADLE SONG

BEES are resting sugary thighs,
Stars awake in the evening skies,
Timothy, Timothy, close your eyes,
    King of the cradle, sleep.

Sleep, my honey ; O sleep, my star,
Dream where the rainbow ribbons are,
Ride with the Queen in the Fairies' car,
    King of the cradle, sleep.

Father is tossing upon the sea,
Timothy rocks at home with me ;
Weary of trumpet, cannon, and knee,
    King of the cradle, sleep.

God, whose babes are many and far,
Keep him from craft, and save from war:
Give to my rose from a golden star,
   Honey and innocent sleep.

You know when mother came just now to kiss us all
    good-night,
She had a lovely necklace on made out of sudden
    light ;
It's just a string of diamonds, and I lie awake to think
What makes each little creature give that blue and
    scarlet wink.

Dick calls them prisoned sunlight, but the sunlight isn't
    blue !
I think him very ignorant to talk like that, don't you ?
O Tommy, wait a moment, for I 'm sure I 've really
    guessed
What has puzzled all the sages in the east and in the
    west.

Now listen.   Very long ago the fairies told the stones
The gossip of the rivers, and the chat of mountain-
    cones ;
But man was never trusted ; so a million gems to-
    night
Are remembering their secrets, and keep winking with
    delight.

THE SLEEPLESS CHILD

I OFTEN cannot sleep at night,
And have the blind up for the light ;
And on the carpet crumbs I put
To tempt the mouse's silky foot.

And then I love to lie and watch
Her feasting in the moonlight patch ;
And if I speak she does not stir,
Because she knows I 'm fond of her.

When sleep outside my bedroom waits,
The mouse and moon are friendly mates,
And if they come they both are sure
To kiss and frolic on the floor.

At p. 42.

TIM'S GRACE

WHEN Baby Tim, who's very small,
Says grace for me, and Nurse, and Paul,
He asks the Lord to make us all
    ' Ter-looly fankful.'

And if we laugh till we are red,
Nurse strokes his sandy-coloured head,
And loves him more because he said
    ' Ter-looly fankful.'

For when he's older, Nursie says,
And grown from all his pretty ways,
She 'll often miss his funny phrase,
    ' Ter-looly fankful.'

THE DEW

HARDLY any youngster knows
What the dew is on a rose.

If you children all are nice
I will teach you in a trice.

Long ago when men were sage,
(This was in the Golden Age,)

They were certain lovely-lipped,
Meadow-haunting fairies tripped

Night by night in starlit reels
Practising their fragile heels.

But to-day to hosts and hosts
Fairies are less real than ghosts.

So at night the fairies weep
While the unbelievers sleep ;

And, while grieving out of view,
Change their sorrow into dew.

Whence, my children, it appears
There 's no salt in fairies' tears !

LOST LABOVR

THERE's a gentleman out yonder
Who is sowing early peas ;
He puts a line across the ground,
And makes a little trench ;
    And already in his folly
    He is feeling very jolly
As he dreams, of coming dinners,
On his knobby rustic bench.

But my artful pouter pigeons
Take great interest in peas,

And they sit devising measures
Which will give that planter pain ;
    For I 'm sure he will be nettled,
    When he hears that they have settled,
And are carefully collecting
All those early peas again.

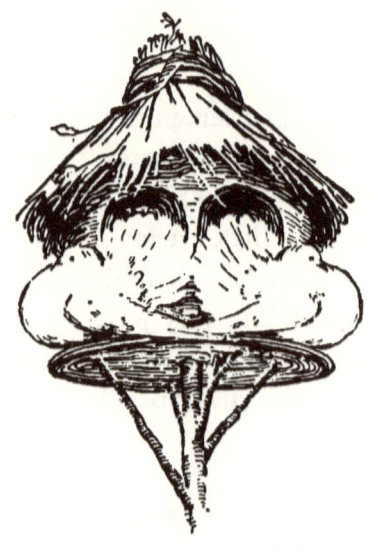

OFF TO THE SEA

HERE comes the train ! Good-bye, Papa ! Good-bye,
    good-bye to all !
We 'll watch you from the window till your bodies grow
    quite small.
They say the engine flies along much faster than a
    bee—
We 're going down to Sherringham to paddle in the
    sea !

Dear Auntie Nell and Nursie, as well as Cousin Mat,
And Noel, grave and chubby, in his ribboned sailor hat,
And Baby, with her merry eyes that sparkle in their
    glee—
We 're going down to Sherringham to paddle in the
    sea !

O run along, dear Puff-puff, just as hard as you can run,
And eat some coal for luncheon while we have our
currant bun,
For Auntie says if you are fed you'll get us there by
three—
We're going down to Sherringham to paddle in the
sea!

At Cromer we shall find a man to drive a wagonette
Past succory and poppies—how we hope it won't be
wet!
And when we reach our lodgings we shall quickly have
our tea—
We're going down to Sherringham to paddle in the
sea!

I mean to build a castle just as tall as Auntie's head
For the waves to knock to pieces when I'm dreaming
in my bed;
And Noel says he'll make a house that's taller than a
tree—
We're going down to Sherringham to paddle in the
sea!

D

Just see the goosey-gander and the moo-cows by the
    brook,
Their sides are marked like those I have at Thetford in
    my book.
O Noel, see the piggies, and the coffee-coloured gee !—
We 're going down to Sherringham to paddle in the
    sea !

And Auntie hopes we 'll freckle on our faces, and be
    brave,
And not cry when Nursie dips us for a minute in the
    wave ;
So I mean to be courageous, as a little girl should be—
We 're going down to Sherringham to paddle in the
    sea !

SILVERWIG'S SIGHT

THERE'S often a rustling by pansy and
    pink,
But what it is rustles I never can
    think;
I hear it and hear it and hear it all day,
And Silverwig says it's the fairies at
    play.

Now Silverwig 's really a very wise boy,
He kisses and strokes the carnations with joy,
And says he can hear all the fairy folks sing
At Puss-in-the-Corner or Kiss-in-the Ring.

They lurk in Sweet-Williams, they crouch in
    the cloves,
They giggle in blooms looking strangely like
    gloves ;
They bend behind pansies, scarce daring to
    wink,
While *He* searches fuschia and violet and
    pink.

In hues of the rainbow they seek and
    they hide,
Some peeping from lilies, some curling
    inside ;
So Silverwig says, and perhaps he is
    right,
For never were eyes so enchanted and
    bright !

How you toddle, sweet and willing,
Hair the colour of a shilling,
    Here to Mammy!
Running in your crumpled pinny,
Have you just escaped from Jenny,
    Silver Sammy?

Now that budded mouth uncloses,
Asking do I want ' sum woses,'
    ' Do 'oo, Mammy?'
Never mind.   I know some letters
That are worries to your betters,
    Silver Sammy!

A THIEF

YOU naughty, naughty, naughty rogue,
    To steal those pretty eggs!
I'm glad to see you pricked your hands
    And scratched your wicked legs.
I never thought my chubby son
    Would like to join those thieves
Who rob the houses of the birds
    Among the thorns and leaves.

These lovely ovals all belong
    To nightingales, not you;
Suppose thieves robbed your nursery
    Of Rose and Dick and Sue—
Suppose they came when Dad was out,
    And found my cosy nest,
Just think of Mother's streaming eyes
    And Father's aching breast!

You left the parent birds one egg?
    That's little comfort, Mick.
Do you imagine nightingales
    Can't do arithmetic?
When robbers steal both you and Rose,
    And take you far from here,
Because they leave me Dick and Sue
    Shall I not notice, dear?

We'll find the cup that held the eggs,
    And pop them in again:
Come, darling, let us run with them
    To save the birds from pain.
If they are out this afternoon,
    I'm sure they soon will come
With eager wings, with sparkling eyes,
    To do their evening sum.

PLAYING AT PARADISE

SHE called to me with dancing eyes,
' We 're both turned out of Paradise ;
The Tree of Knowledge was the pear,
That 's over in the corner there.

' And, mother dearest, Cousin Jake
Was simply splendid as the snake ;
He curved about the trunk ; to hiss
He shot his tongue out, just like this.

' He kicked the branches with his feet,
To knock us down some pears to eat,
And when we tasted them there came
An angel with a sword of flame.

'Bob was the angel ; and he said
We must dig thistles for our bread.
And though we digged with toil and pain,
He'd make the thistles grow again.

'But can he, mother?   And he says
The orchard's shut to us for days.
Do come, and make him let us in,
Because we're sorry for our sin.'

I went ; and whirling by the gate
A wooden sword about his pate
I found our Bob in angel-wise
Guarding his orchard-paradise.

'Beware the flaming sword !' he cried,
'It turns all ways!   Don't come inside!'
'Now, Bob, run in,' I laughing said,
'It's time all angels went to bed.'

TO SHARP

Now, Sharp, I admit that those troublesome geese
Were the very worst foes for my
    early Spring peas,
But I must say I grieve for this
    gander's decease,
  You remarkably truculent lurcher.

If dogs have a Prophet, a possible
    fact,
He surely prescribes how your kin-
    dred should act,
And I feel very certain he advo-
    cates tact,
  You remarkably truculent lurcher.

To pull out a feather or so from behind
Would teach even goslings their manners
    to mind ;
And a goose to such warnings is never
    quite blind,
  You remarkably truculent lurcher.

But chasing a goose to the
shed by the stack,
And killing him there in
that dark *cul de sac*,
Displays of forgiveness a
terrible lack,
You remarkably trucu-
lent lurcher.

I whistled and shouted till, growing
quite hoarse,
I thumped with my stick as a final
resource ;
But I cannot admit that you showed
much remorse,
You remarkably truculent lurcher.

Now Farmer Treherne, in a note
cold as frost,
Has sent me a bill for the bird he
has lost ;
Nine shillings and sixpence your
butchery cost,
You remarkably truculent
lurcher.

When honoured next time by a visit from geese,
Allow me to say, and to emphasize, please,
That I really prefer them to damage my peas,
    You remarkably truculent lurcher.

THE THANKFUL BIRD

Now I—yellowhammer—
  Desire to give praise
For plentiful orchards
  And sunshiny days :
The Spring gave me many
  A bud for my bill,
And sent me a sweetheart
  From over the hill.

She lent me a rose-bush
  Along by the quick,
And there I was minstrel
  To mother and chick ;
The leaves were our shutters,
  The thorns were our bars,
When nested in blossoms
  We slept under stars.

Though winter that changes
  My music and gold
Is big on the hillside
  And brave on the wold,

By Mercy remembered,
By Tenderness fed,
The hedge is my larder,
The hip is my bread.

THE LOST LAMB

YOUR mother, lamb,
    Will not forsake you ;
No leering wolf
    Shall overtake you.

With other lambs
    You frisked, forgetting
Your woolly mother's
    Voice and petting.

So now your heart
    With fear is beating ;
You fill the air
    With constant bleating.

And I am sure
   Your mother's crying;
She thinks you lost,
   Or dead, or dying.

So stay, my dear,
   Both fond and steady,
Where milk and love
   Are always ready.

E

THE · RAINBOW ·

THREE fairies climbed a rainbow hill ;
And two were Jacks, and one a Jill.

Each clambered up a coloured lane,
In pleasure dreaming not of pain.

At last the heavenly beamy belt
Began in lessening love to melt ;

Whereat the fairies through the arch
Fell headlong in a wood of larch.

Each, being hurt in leg and arm,
Was carried to a fairies' farm,

Where comrades gave them creamy milk,
And dressed their wounds in softest silk.

A doctor came, who smiled and said,
A rainbow was less safe than bed.

So this the moral you must scan—
Not where you wish, but where you can.

A QUESTION

HERE on the down where the sea-wind is bleak,
Blowing our voices away as we speak,
Stands the grey shepherd with collie and crook,
Reading the sky as a page from a book.

Sheep to the westward and sheep to the east,
Spindle-legged, shivering, recently fleeced !
Shepherd of ewes looking shameful and sad,
Have you as many as Abraham had ?

At p. 69.

AUNT·JAN

WHEN Aunt Jan's coming there's such romping in the
house,
She's sweeter than a daffodil and softer than a mouse!
She sings about the passages, and never wants to
rest,
And father says it's all because a bird is in her breast.

When Aunt Jan's kissing there's such crowding round
her knees,
Such clambers to her bosom, and such battles for a
squeeze!
We dirty both her snowy cuffs, we trample on her gown,
And sometimes all her yellow hair comes tumbling
tumbling down.

When Aunt Jan's dancing we all watch her as she goes,
With in-and-out and round-about upon her shiny toes;
And when her merry breath is tired she stops the fun
    and stands
To curtsy saucily to us, or kiss her pretty hands.

When Aunt Jan's playing, the piano seems alive,
With all the notes as busy as the bees are in a hive;
And when it's time for Bedfordshire, as sweetly as a lark
She sings that God is waiting to protect us in the dark.

When Aunt Jan's leaving we are not ashamed to cry,
A-kissing at the station and a-waving her good-bye;
But springtime brings the crocus after winter rain and
    frost,
So dear Aunt Jan will come again. She isn't really lost.

East & West

ALL the men of the West are here
With gauntlet, pipeclay, horse, and spear;
All the men of the East are come
With bugle, standard, fife, and drum.

Though each may bluster like a foe,
I do not think much blood will flow;
But every man of the West, at least,
Will stare very hard at the men from the East.

You all remember father's looks
When you have inked his pretty books;
Such stares will pierce each scarlet breast,
And stab the hearts of the men from the West.

If they are wise they will delight
In peace, for only sillies fight :
'Tis best that they should take the train
For home and mother's kiss again.

THE VIOLIN

VIOLET, Mary, Dick, come in !
    Daddy's taken the violin ;
And he's going to play for you and me
    The tune of the Bonnets of Bonnie Dundee !

He's tucked the fiddle under his chin,
    He says he's ready to begin ;
And when Dundee has ridden away
    He'll fiddle us over the Emerald Bay !

He'll trip us into County Clare,
    And dance us over the Bridge of the Air.
Violet, Mary, Dick, come in !
    Daddy's taken the violin !

A LULLABY

Sleep, my angels, side by side
  Till the morrow's coming,
Till the rosebuds open wide
  At the brown bees' humming;

Angel rosebuds, dream and wait
  Till the sun is peeping
At my maid and at her mate,
  Rosebud angels, sleeping.

Seraphina

Now the babies are in bed,
Seraphina, you can rest ;
You can lick that furry fist,
    Wash that snowy breast.

Little time those cherubs give
For a cleanly habit's scope,
Kitten using neither sponge,
    Water-jug, nor soap.

When you want refreshment,
    puss,
Run along with tabby face,
Dip moustaches in the milk,
    Softly purring grace.

Singing then melodious love,
Voice your satisfaction deep,
Till the friendly food and fire
    Make you go to sleep.

WHY, Mother, it surely is time
   That Timothy here was transplanted
To a sheety and blankety clime,
   Where his presence is, more or less, wanted.

I admit he's an angel, of course,
   But I wish that your rules were more drastic;
I object, as a fatherly horse,
   To a bit of uncleanly elastic.

He has fashioned and fixed at my ears
   Ridiculous papery blinkers,
And I'm sure my condition appears
   `Sufficiently foolish to thinkers.

As another inducement, I urge
   That his driving's distinctly immoral,
All affectionate feeling I merge
   When he thumps on my head with his coral.

Moreover, my study 's too small
  To allow of superb demivolting,
So I think (there will be a great squall!)
  Of unseating my rider, and bolting!

To be spurred by a pin is too bad ;
  I prefer to be driver, not driven—
Yes, dearest, I know that the lad
  Is a cherub levanted from Heaven,

But since he intends to remain
  In our semi-detached little mansion,
I think, to avoid future pain,
  We should govern his moral expansion.

So ring for the nursemaid, my dear,
  (Tim, Tim, make an end of that screaming!)
For the cherub must now disappear
  To his tub, to his blankets and dreaming.

OVER all the world I 'll tramp
Till I find Aladdin's Lamp :
When I have it, I shall keep
In my rabbit-hutch, asleep,

Black of hair and bright of eye,
Willing at my slightest cry,
Quick to vanish, big and brave,
Such a Genie for my slave !

Then if any robbers come,
Searching in our sleepy home,
Tho' the silver spoons they take,
I shan't worry when I wake.

ALADDIN'S LAMP

Anything that mother wants
Must be fetched from farthest haunts,
Sinbad's valley, plain or hill,
For the Genie has the skill.

Mother says that Persia's rose
Sweetens more than Europe knows,
So, of course, my slave will run
Picking out the finest one!

OFF TO AFRICA

THE cuckoos of the neighbourhood are meeting in the
    park,
They mean to journey leagues away before the day falls
    dark.
Oh, sweet their stay in England, and the music from their
    beak,
But now they flit to Africa, because their chests are weak.

In counties such as Warwick, if they wintered they
    would die,
Speckled children of the sunbeam in a bluer, brighter
    sky ;
But they visit us in springtime just to fly about and
    speak,
Ere they point away to Africa, because their chests are
    weak.

Though they treat the hedge-birds badly, we forgive
    them for their note,
For their mellow bar of beauty, for their finely feathered
    coat ;
They are parents of an order not affectionate, nor
    meek,
These cuckoos bound for Africa, because their chests
    are weak.

Though they fly away from England over many a weary
    mile,
They love our caterpillars and they like our cosy isle.
These gentlemen in feathers, with their ladies fair and
    fleet,
When Spring is green, will travel here to call across the
    wheat.

So at parting we God-speed them with no reprehend-
    ing word,
Dear guests for our civility—there goes the pilot bird !
Farewell till wood-anemones are friendly by the creek—
We spare you all for Africa, because your chests are
    weak.

FAIRIES IN FACES

I LIKE to sit on Daddy's knee,
 And watch the fairy in his face,
That always has a smile for me,
 And never wanders from her place.

And mother says the eyes of Joy
 Will make a thousand faces shine,
When Love can spare each little boy
 A father half as sweet as mine.

THE WALLS OF JERICHO

Bob, Jake, and Harry, Tim and Dick,
Each blowing on a trumpet-stick,
Must walk all round as valiant knights
Among the beardy Israelites.

And blow, and blow like anything,
Till all the sandy deserts ring ;
For down will topple, if you blow,
The fortress walls of Jericho.

These boxes shall the city be,
And Jane, the cook, has lent them me ;
And mother says this scarlet rag
On Daddy's stick can be the flag.

Minnie and I, within the town
Shall be the grizzled guards to frown;
And when the Israelitish host
Is puffing out its cheeks the most,

Then we inside will kick the wall,
And down each orange-box will fall
In just the way that, long ago,
There tumbled towers in Jericho!

INNOCENCY

NOEL likes to go to sleep with roses in his fingers ;
All around his darling mouth a love for blossom lingers.
Moonlit birds upon the thorn, and stars with golden
   carol,
Sing while fairies dance for him in wonderland apparel.

Rose, and star, and nightingale, and fairies round him
   leaping,
Travel with him, fill his heart, or wide awake or sleeping !
If from out an older breast he banishes you never,
Mother will be sure of him for ever and for ever.

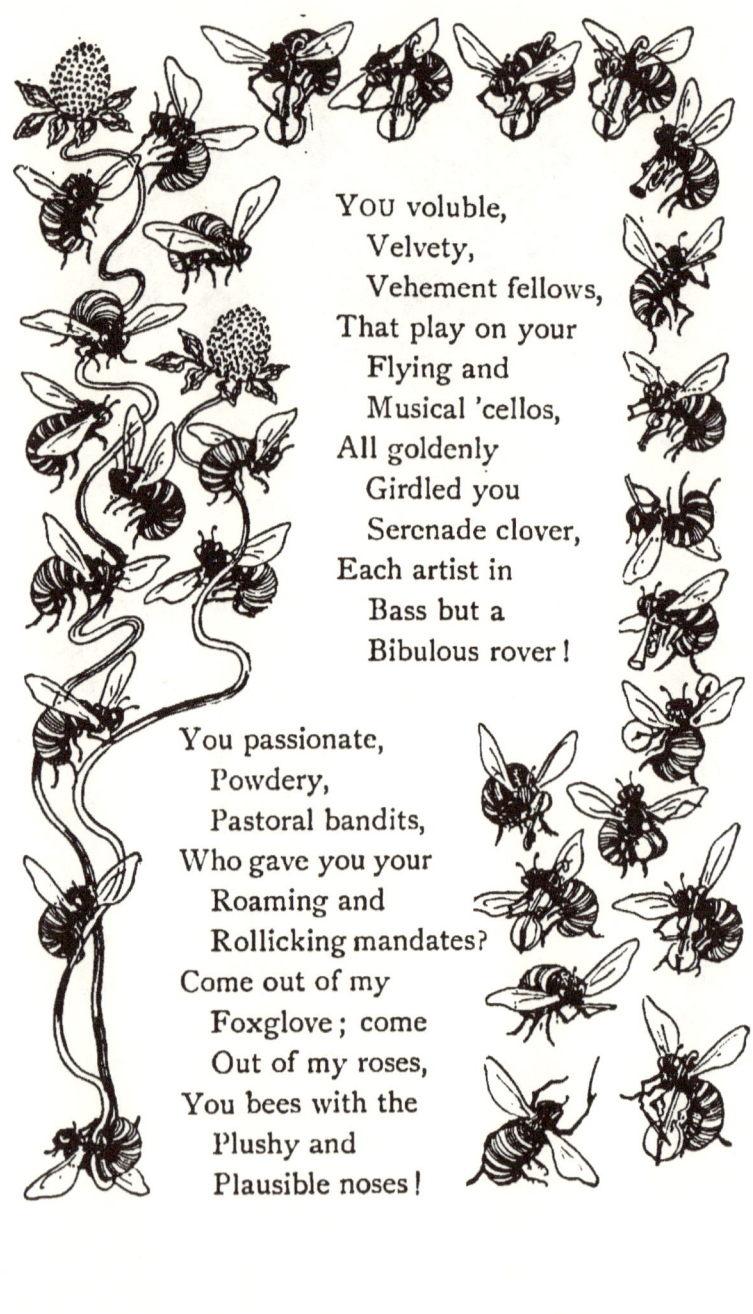

You voluble,
　Velvety,
　Vehement fellows,
That play on your
　Flying and
　Musical 'cellos,
All goldenly
　Girdled you
　Serenade clover,
Each artist in
　Bass but a
　Bibulous rover !

You passionate,
　Powdery,
　Pastoral bandits,
Who gave you your
　Roaming and
　Rollicking mandates?
Come out of my
　Foxglove; come
　Out of my roses,
You bees with the
　Plushy and
　Plausible noses !

LATE FOR TEA

HERE'S Auntie all ready and sitting in silk,
With cakes on the table and lots of new milk,
So, Mou-Mou, be quick as a fairy would be,
Pop on a clean pinny, and run down to tea!

For Noel is keeping his eye on the cake,
And after his blessing what havoc he'll make!
So, Mou-Mou, be quick as a fairy would be,
Pop on a clean pinny, and run down to tea!

Dear Baby has given that sweet little nod,
Which her golden head makes when she murmurs
  'Tank God.'
So, Mou-Mou, be quick as a fairy would be,
Pop on a clean pinny, and run down to tea!

At p. 89.

SYDDIE

You love to wander in the dew,
    Caring not for patter of the showers
And sweet it is to meet with you,
    Syddie, with your pinny full of flowers.

You gather pinks, but cannot take
    Hollyhocks that grow as tall as towers;
But others reach them for your sake,
    Syddie, with your pinny full of flowers.

Who kisses you in early Spring,
    Kisses with the cowslips of the showers.
When I am weary, Summer, bring
    Syddie, with his pinny full of flowers.

BEDFORDSHIRE

ITALIAN stories we have read,
  Now, merry hearts, be off to bed!
Say your prayers with heads bent down,
  Pop into each flannel gown.
When mother brings the good-night sweet,
  And tucks the clothes about your feet,
Then sink to rest; then ready be
  To dream of doves in Tuscany.

Here's chocolate for Tiny Tim,
  Rob's not forgot, there's some for him!
Open that rosebud, Dorothy,
  And taste how sweet Mamma can be!
To-morrow we will have a swing,
  Or kiss the cowslips by the spring;
To-night be busy, one, two, three,
  With dreams of doves in Tuscany.

Ah, nurse, how quick they are to weep,
  Or melt from noisy romps to sleep!
Most precious faces in the world,
  Rose-brown from sun, and golden curled!
As life o'ertakes them with surprise,
  Stay, Innocency, in their eyes,
And keep their hearts a long time free
  To dream of doves in Tuscany.

THE STUFFED MAGPIES

IN the days when I was happy with my childish loves
    and games,
With my mother's quick caresses that forgave my
    simple shames,
In my room (the eyes of memory can see the very
    place!)
There were perching two stuffed magpies in an old
    glass case.

When I grew to want of daring, I adventured on the
    sea,
And I started from my mother's kiss half tearful, half
    in glee;

But often from the Tropics all my heart would fly apace
To my mother and the little room that held the old
    glass case.   •

Then at last my feet turned homeward to the farmstead
    and the stack,
But mother dear was gone away, and never could come
    back.
The furniture remained ; and oh, the tears that stung
    my face
When I saw the two stuffed magpies in the old glass
    case !

Father Thrush

THE thrush was a bachelor early in March,
And now there's a wife with a velvety heart;
 There's a house in the quick
 Never builded of brick,
And a capital egg for a start.

The thrush was a bachelor early in March,
And now there's a medley of bosom and bill!
 There are Susan and Dick
 In the daggers of quick,
And a couple of golden-throats still!

THE SWAN

SEE the swan go
In his jacket of snow,
An island of white
In a lake of delight.

See the swan swim,
When I scatter for him
The half of my cake
On the top of the lake.

See the swan glide
To the bank's rushy side,
So suddenly fleet
By the strokes of his feet.

See the swan lie
In the blue of the sky;
And under his breast
Another at rest!

THANKS

THANK you very much indeed,
River, for your waving reed ;
Mr. Sun, for jolly beam ;
Mrs. Cow, for milk and cream;
Hollyhocks, for budding knobs ;
Foxgloves, for your velvet fobs ;
Pansies, for your silky cheeks ;
Chaffinches, for singing beaks ;
Spring, for wood anemones
Near the mossy toes of trees ;
Summer, for the fruited pear,
Yellowing crab and cherry fare ;

Autumn, for the bearded load,
Hazel-nuts along the road ;
Winter, for the fairy tale,
Spitting log and bouncing hail ;
Christmas Day, for Mary's Child,
Jesus manifest and mild.

But, blest Father high above,
All these joys are from your love ;
And your children everywhere,
Born in palace, lane, or square,
Cry, with voices all agreed,
THANK YOU VERY MUCH INDEED!

THE OFFENDED SNAIL

A SNAIL, when climbing up a rose,
By thorns assaulted, pricked her nose.
She dropped, and wrote with painful scrawl
A silver sentence on the wall.

A fairy who was wondrous wise
Regarded this with beamy eyes,
And straightway with a lovely laugh
Announced the glazy autograph.

' A rose,' the shelly scribe had writ,
' May be the very spice of wit;
But 'tis not comely with a thorn
To greet a lady's offered horn ! '

IN ARABIA

In a far Arabian glen
Cousin Bob conducted Ben.
How they went from Hamp-
    stead Heath
No one knoweth—no one saith.
Then began in field and lane
Strange adventures thick as
    rain,
For a fountain played in air,
And it had no bottom there.
Flashed along the upright pool
Rainbow lights most beautiful ;
Every spray of water sang
Till the glade's seclusion rang
With such music as the stars
Send abroad in lovely bars.

Next they trod a precious
    mould,
Where each spear of grass was
    gold,

And, as far as they could view,
Diamonds served in place of dew.
Crickets, lizards, adders, birds,
Antelopes in antlered herds,
Buffaloes with opal eyes,
Bees, sweet-heavy at the thighs,
Leopards crouching for the spring,
Eagles of the hissing wing,

All, and more than I have told,
Shaped divinely were from gold.

Passing all these marvels by,
Next a forest touched the sky ;
Hand-in-hand the children, mute,
Gazed in wonder at the fruit,
For the branches bent with gems
Fit for finest diadems.

Here were topaz-orchards ; there
Emeralds hanging in the air,
Rubies as great apples big,
Sapphires larger than a fig :
When the breeze spoke, low and sweet,
Pearls kept pattering round their feet ;
Never yet did forest bear
Stones so radiant as grew there.

When they passed the onyx tree,
Chrysolite, chalcedony,
Straight they found beyond the wood
Wonder in another mood.
For, as still as warriors slain,
Thousands slumbered on the plain ;
All a deadly silence kept,
Elephants and camels slept,
Not a hound that twitched an ear,
As the children's tread came near ;
Negro servants, black as soot,
Never stirred a dusky foot ;
All the army tricked for fight
Slumbered deeply as the night,
And the plume upon his cap
Fluttered o'er the general's map.

Mute the trumpets wont to blare,
Breaking up the startled air;
Even vultures in the sky
Hung asleep, and could not fly.
Bob began to cry aloud,
Lo, a dropping of the cloud,

And a genie from the mist
Nursing lightning in his fist!
Far and wide rang Bobby's scream—
.   .   .   .   .
Auntie says it was a dream.

AUNTIE NELL

WE have to stay in bed
  Till Auntie comes up-stairs ;
And then we cluster round her knees
  To say our prayers.

And after asking God
  To keep us good and sweet,
Dear Nursie does her very best
  To make us neat.

But if we go a walk,
  Or ride the pony Bell,
It is not fun unless we have
  Our Auntie Nell.

At p. 104.

We look in every room,
    But Mother is not there;
She's never, never in the house,
    Or anywhere.

Yet, Daddy says, some day
    We'll find her bright and well;
Till then we must contrive to do
    With Auntie Nell.

THANK GOD

WHEN Baby settles in his place,
With folded hands he says his grace—
    Thank God!

The porridge has no time to cool.
Dad calls it brief and beautiful—
    Thank God!

For father, kinder ev'ry year,
For mother hasting to be near,
    Thank God!

For Baby Timothy so sweet,
For flowers to pick, for bread to eat,
    Thank God!

There really is not more to say
Than this by night as well as day—
    Thank God!

Voyaging

HERE ye have reached at the end of the day,
Over the opal and emerald bay,
Half of it breakers and half of it beams,
The harbour of dreams.

Each of ye saw, as ye sailed to the port,
Dolphins at tumble and seabirds at sport;
Now shall ye rest, and shall drop in the deep
The anchor of sleep.

Then when the sunbeams are gay on the boat,
Up, my adventurers, farther to float!
Crowd on your mast, if ye cruise for delight,
The canvas of flight.

PARENTS

BEFORE SLEEP

How better, Father, could we pray
Than thus at end of honest day,
Naked at heart, without pretence,
Secure in simple excellence,
A wife and husband, hand in hand,
At prayers among the sleeping band
Of angels whom Thy love hath lent
To bind our household sacrament?

When better, Father, could we ask
Thy care than after righteous task,
The need well met, the dream refused,
The oil not spilled, the clean lamp used?
Two grey-haired children kneel to Thee,
In suit for fresh felicity,
Whose married worship to Thine ear,
Allowed, parental, rises clear.

Nor wealth, nor place as gifts Divine
I ask to fall on sons of mine;
But, most of all, a nature sure
To share the heart with rich and poor.
O give them tears! O make them feel
An inward energy to heal,
That never, full of frosty pride,
They pass upon the other side.

Behold these children, Father, God,
Their strip of life so briefly trod;

Their hearts unshaded by the gloom,
Their eyes scarce looking past a bloom.
To act as ministers in these
Implant such holy qualities
That they may march with love unspent,
And in Thy discipline content.

www.ingramcontent.com/pod-product-compliance
Lightning Source LLC
Chambersburg PA
CBHW020408030726
47496CB00007B/2365